Arabian Lights

Book Six

Tricia Martin

The Old Tree Series

Book One
The Old Tree

Book Two
The Land of Bizia

Book Three
The Kingdom of Knon

Book Four
The Mild, Mild West

Book Five
Into the Night Sky

Book Six
The Arabian Lights

Book Seven
One for All and All for One

Request for information
Contact Tricia Martin at
tricia.martin@soulbreakthru.com

To Michael Martin
Because of your love for reading,
especially fantasy adventures,
this series is dedicated to you.
Someday you will give these stories
to your own children to read,
and that will make me laugh
with joy.

Contents

Arabian Lights
Book Six

Tricia Martin

Chapter One

The Old Tree

This story takes place many years ago when your parents were children. Videogames hadn't been invented yet or cell phones, and television had only six or seven channels.

Eddie and his sister, Audrey, were sitting in their living room, looking out the front window. They had a lovely window seat with home-sewn cushions on it and a perfect view of the rural countryside that surrounded them.

They lived in Southern Orange County, which was known as Mission Viejo. At that time, there were orange trees everywhere in the county: groves and groves of them grew up and down Southern California.

Eddie was eleven, and his sister, Audrey, was ten years old. There were very few homes in their neighborhood, which made it perfect for playing games outside and having make-believe adventures. It was summer-time, and after sitting looking out the window and trying to decide what to do, they went outside into the sunshine and fresh air to play among the trees and open land near their home.

"Let's imagine we're astronauts, and we've landed on another planet," yelled Eddie from behind a large tree. "Look around for a good rocket ship."

"Okay. Then I can be the first girl astronaut!" Straightening her pigtails, Audrey thought about what it would be like to walk on another planet.

Eddie circled several trees, examining them closely. Suddenly, he stopped. "Hey, come here."

"What?" Audrey gasped for breath as she sprinted to the tree. "What is it?"

"Look!" Eddie's pointed to the tree.

"What? Oh! O-o-h! That's strange." She stared at the old tree with its brilliant colors that even her brand-new television set couldn't imitate. The trunk was an unusual brown that seemed to vibrate with life, and the greens were so much greener than the other trees surrounding it. She decided she was looking at the real thing for the first time: a beautiful, colorful, living tree.

"That's strange. I've never noticed this tree here and we've played in this area before." Eddie looked at the old tree again.

"Well, it's perfect for our space-craft, already looks out of this world." Eddie laughed a fresh, hearty laugh and threw his head back to look up through the branches. "Ever seen anything like this? Don't know much about nature and trees, but this is really different."

"You're right. It's very strange. The colors really stand out." Audrey examined the old tree again. Suddenly, she heard a noise, muffled, but it seemed to be coming from around the base of the trunk. Eddie heard it too and moved closer to Audrey. As she studied the tree trunk, a small crack appeared and grew wider and wider.

She realized the crack was now large enough for a boy or girl to crawl through, if they got down on their knees.

Eddie looked at her and then studied the old tree thoughtfully. "I think we can squeeze through that opening. Looks big enough. I'm game if you are?"

Audrey felt irritated. It was just like her brother to leave this decision up to her. Studying the old tree, she frowned at him and felt hesitant and cautious about this new situation.

She examined the tree again and

said, "I hate it when you do this. Do you want me to make this decision?"

Eddie looked confused. "Just giving you a choice."

"I know I'll regret this. You go first. It's your idea anyway."

"You know the saying: ladies first." Eddie laughed.

"I'm not a lady. I'm a girl, and I need you to lead."

"Can't you take a joke? Get a sense of humor, sis, and would I lead you into anything dangerous? Okay, don't answer that."

Eddie threw himself down on his knees and crawled into the opening in the trunk. Audrey waited a minute to see if he would yell and come crawling back out, but he disappeared inside.

She lowered herself slowly onto her knees and crawled through the opening. Relieved to find the interior of the tree quite roomy, she stood up inside. There was a wonderful scent of fresh-cut grass and the fragrance of flowers all blending together in the interior.

She had expected to be cramped and crowded inside the tree but was surprised to find she was in a spacious room. Grass covered the entire floor, with tiny, delicate flowers of every color planted around the edge. The interior walls were smooth and dry and softly lit by a source that filtered down from above their heads.

"The inside's bigger than the outside. How strange! And there are no bugs in here, at least none I can see. It's quite nice, Eddie."

"See, told you it'd be all right. I know about these things."

Audrey looked around with a smile on her face. "Yeah, you know how to get us into trouble, but this time it looks okay."

Eddie brushed the grass from his knees, and Audrey did the same. Surveying their surroundings, they found a table in the corner with several chairs.

As they were looking at the table, Audrey noticed something happening to the far wall, opposite where they had entered. It was being altered in some way. Eddie must have noticed too, because he walked toward it and found a door had taken shape in the far wall, slightly open.

"Well, Audrey, this is more fun than our imaginary adventure. We've stumbled on the real thing. No idea what's on the other side; but I have a feeling that if we walk through, something exciting's waiting for us. What do you think?"

Audrey was quiet for a moment and then said, "there you go again, making me decide. Okay, let's go, but *you* lead the way." She felt her heart pounding, and her hands were sweaty.

Leaning forward, she watched as Eddie placed his hand on the silver doorknob.

Chapter Two

The World of Sand

When the door opened, Audrey peered into darkness. Eddie stepped through first, and she followed, being careful not to shut the door (you never know when you may need to exit quickly).

At first, she thought something had happened to her vision. Unable to see clearly, she realized they had arrived in the dead of night.

Gradually, her eyes adjusted to the darkness all around her. A faint light shone out from the tree's interior onto sand. *Wonder if we've landed on a beach.* She grabbed Eddie's hand as they moved further into the new world. When she looked back, soft light spilled out of the door, out-lining its shape and the surrounding sand. *Good, the door's still open.*

Audrey looked around. "Okay! I've had enough. Time to go home." She shivered as she moved back toward the doorway, and her voice gave away the uneasiness she was feeling. "Can't just bumble around in the dark with no idea of where, when, or what place we're in." She pulled on Eddie's hand, indicating the direction she wished to go.

"It's all right, Audrey. Have I ever led you into any dangerous situation?"

"Well, now that you mention it, there was the time—" Before she could finish, a shrill howl broke the silence. A strong, cold wind blew around them, making her shiver again, and then a loud slam sounded behind her.

Audrey did not want to turn around. She was afraid that the door to the old tree had made the loud noise and now they were trapped in this dark, strange land.

Finally mustering up her courage, she turned around and her fears were realized. The door and light that had shone through it were both gone. A chill went down her back, and she shivered one more time in the cold.

Eddie took off his jacket and placed it over her trembling shoulders in an effort to warm her up. He put his arm around her. He had always been a good older brother, protective and kind. But he did have a way of taking them into one crazy adventure after another.

Audrey decided this was the weirdest one yet.

"Don't worry, sis. I'll figure something out, always do." Eddie scuffed up her hair and smiled.

Of course, she couldn't see the smile, but she heard it in the tone of his voice. Allowing herself to relax, she felt warmer inside. But where were they?

From somewhere in the distance came a pounding noise and animal grunts. Then lights appeared in the distance. Over a sand dune in front of them, Audrey could see shapes moving rapidly toward them, but there was nowhere to hide. All they could do was stand and wait, hoping that with a little luck, the darkness would conceal them.

Well, luck was not with them that night. Audrey felt instinctively that the people galloping toward them were a group of bandits, cutthroats, and robbers. She stood bravely, with Eddie at her side, facing the sandstorm as it barreled down on them.

It didn't take long for the pack to reach them, and Audrey stared into the darkness at the band of thieves that now encircled her, their torches blazing in the black night. Thirty to forty dirty men on horseback surrounded them, and the smell of horses and humans mixed in the night air.

The strangers had rough cloth wrapped around their heads. Some wore these turbans tied in the back while others had them wrapped loosely, allowing the material to fall around their faces and shoulders. They were dress in layered clothing with tunics over the top, and all carried rifles.

The brown horses had small rugs thrown over their backs, and they looked well taken care of and healthy. They snorted and stomped their hoofs impatiently as the riders pulled back on their reins to quiet them.

The expression on the faces of the thieves was serious, hardened, and cold. In response, Audrey grabbed her brother's hand, squeezed tightly and shivered again. Waves of dizziness rolled over her, but she grabbed

Eddie's arm to steady herself.

The leader of the group said something to her and Eddie, but it wasn't in English. He stared hard at them, waited, and then motioned for a few of his men to follow his orders.

Three young, smelly, dusty bandits slid off their horses and swaggered over to them. Grabbing Audrey roughly, they tied her hands together with coarse rope, pushing her toward the horses. She could hear the leader barking orders in another language, and she was thankful she didn't understand what was being said.

Her wrists stung where the rope bit into her skin. The young bandits shoved her up against one of the horses. To her relief, when she looked up, her brother was standing in front of another horse near her.

He smiled and winked. "Don't worry, sis. We'll get out of this. I promise you," he whispered.

Eddie had always reassured her in scary situations, but this was beyond anything they'd ever experienced before. She felt sick and faint again, but comfort came from knowing her brother was there beside her.

One of the men picked her up and threw her roughly onto the back of a horse. She watched as her brother was thrown on the back of the horse next to her. The bandits took off with such force that she had to grab her rider's tunic tightly or she would surely have fallen off.

Gradually, her eyes became accustomed to the shadowy night, and twinkling stars shone down from the sky. Audrey looked up. She was amazed at the beauty of the night sky and how brightly the lights shone down on her, and it comforted her greatly. She thought back to stories about stars leading the way to important events in history.

Please watch over us, she whispered as she gazed up at the sparkling stars looking down on her and her brother. Her shivering stopped, and she felt warmth fill her. She was not alone, and she could sense a presence near to her; someone in the heavens was watching over her and would take care of her and her brother. As she looked up again at the night sky, several stars seemed to wink back at her, as if to say, *Don't be afraid. We will help you.*

Chapter Three

The Bandits

They rode through the night for what seemed like hours. Eddie stared hard into the darkness. He could make out shadowy shapes that appeared to be sand dunes covering the land.

Finally, the group slowed down and entered a rough campsite with simple black tents scattered every-where and a fire blazing in the center of the camp.

Someone grabbed Eddie harshly, pulled him off his horse, and threw him to the ground in such a way that he was not injured. He heard a thump beside him and turned his head just in time to see Audrey thrown down next to him.

He studied the desert campsite surrounding them. Goats wandered in and out of the tents, and camels were tied up to stakes, chewing away at something.

Watching the camels chew, he suddenly felt a grumbling in his own stomach and realized he hadn't eaten in a while. He knew a meal was being prepared by the aroma that drifted toward him.

Looking hopefully over at the fire, he wasn't surprised to see an old, worn-out coffee pot sitting warming. Next to it was a rusted, dusty oven from which the desert dwellers periodically removed what looked and smelled like roasted meat. He found out later it was lamb, but the delicious aroma at that moment was driving him crazy.

They were left on their own while the bandits moved over to the food, and Eddie wondered if he and his sister would be offered any.

"You okay, Audrey?" He whispered as he looked around.

"Yes, I'm better now. Finally stopped shaking. While we were on horseback, something happened that calmed me down." She stopped talking when one of the bandits looked over in their direction.

After several hours, a young man walked toward them and shoved an old metal cup in their hands. Eddie saw that it was filled with a green hot liquid. He found a way to hold the cup with his hands tied. When he took a sip, it tasted like coffee that was heavily spiced but warmed his whole body, and he was grateful for that. He wondered if this brew came from the coffeepot he had seen on the stove.

Audrey was having a hard time holding the cup upright and spilled some of the hot liquid down her shirt. After watching Eddie, with her hands still tied, she was able to put the cup to her lips and drink.

The men ate their fill, talked and laughed boisterously, and then began to move away from the fire. The talk and laughter died as they stumbled into their tents, but a few lay down where they were and went to sleep immediately.

Then the same young man came over and threw a metal plate on the ground next to them with the leftover meat that Eddie had been smelling for several hours. Eddie held up his hands in front of the young man, showing the ropes tied around his wrists. Pulling out a knife, the bandit cut the ropes, enabling Eddie and Audrey to grab the food in front of them. Eddie stuffed the meat into his mouth, grateful to be finally eating.

"What are we going to do?" whispered Audrey with desperation in her voice. She rubbed her wrists gently, grateful to have them free from the painful rope.

"We're going to eat! Boy, this

meat's good. I remember studying these desert dwellers in school—they like roast lamb. Think that's what we're eating."

Audrey looked at him with disbelief in her eyes. "Amazing—you're focusing on your stomach at a time like this."

"What? We have to eat. And I'm starving!"

She fell silent, grabbed some of the roast lamb and turned her back to him, but he could see she was finally eating. After both had finished, they sat for a long time listening to the camp sounds.

Audrey broke the quiet. "It would be nice to have soap and water to wash my hands; eating this way is so messy. Have you noticed the dust and dirt? And I don't remember sand looking like this."

"So you've decided to talk to me. Sorry about earlier, but we'll need to keep up our strength. Food's a good thing to have right now."

"You're right. But I'm tired and frightened."

"It's going to all work out. You'll see." But Eddie wondered if it really would work out this time.

He examined the campsite. Everyone was in tents or asleep near the firepit, and silence filled the night air.

Suddenly, Audrey turned to her brother. "Did you hear that?"

"What?"

"There it goes again. Sounds like a baby crying, but what would a baby be doing here?"

Eddie had seen no women or children in the group. "You're probably hearing an animal." But he became alert and began to listen more intently.

After what seemed like ages, another dirty young man came over and partially dragged, partially walked them to a tent made of a rough, dark cloth. He dumped them in front of the door flap and then walked into a nearby tent.

As Eddie pulled the flap open, he jumped back in reaction to the foul odor pouring out of the doorway. It smelled like rotten eggs, garbage and dirty diapers all rolled into one. He remembered his flashlight in his pocket, and pulling it out and turned to Audrey.

"Let's see what kind of place we've landed in."

He moved through the flap into the tent and shone the light around the inside. Over in the corner were several old mattresses and quilts that badly needed to be washed. But what caught his gaze was a crude little cradle in the corner of the tent. Both Eddie and Audrey rushed over to the cradle and looked down. Gazing up at them was a tiny baby, half-naked, lying quietly in a dirty bed.

Audrey turned to her brother. "I think he's been kidnapped!" She placed her hand on the baby's head. "Looks well fed but this cradle's filthy. Poor little thing. Don't worry. I'll find you some clothes to wear."

She searched around the filthy tent and found several small blankets and wrapped the baby in them.

"Best I can do. Sorry, little one, these are more rags than blankets." The baby looked up at her and smiled. She placed him gently back in the cradle.

"Now what would these raiders

want with a little baby? I think you're right about him being kidnapped. They could get money from his parents." Mike looked concerned.

Looking down at the tiny face, he could see the baby was alert and watching them.

"You're a cute little thing." Audrey placed her finger in the baby's hand, and he held it tightly.

Eddie looked up to see the young man who had put them in the tent, standing in the opening. He motioned to Audrey and pointed to the baby and then held up something he was carrying in his arms. It was an ice chest.

The young nomad moved into the tent and put the ice chest down, pointing to the baby again. He opened it and handed Audrey what looked like milk and a bottle.

"Think he wants me to feed it." Audrey smiled at the infant and tenderly picked him up and rocked him. After she filled the bottle with milk, she placed it in the baby's mouth and began to sing softly. The man grunted approvingly and left.

"It's strange-looking milk, but he must be used to it. Look how he gulps it down." Audrey poured a small amount into her cupped hand and licked it. "Tastes different than cow's milk."

"Probably because it's goat's milk. Remember that paper I did on the desert? Goats are more common here than cows." Eddie turned back from his sister to the baby. "Look how he likes it."

"Well, that problem's solved. I was wondering what the little guy was going to eat." She slowly rocked the baby in her arms. "Think I'll call you David. What do you think?"

Her brother looked down at the tiny face. "Yep, I think David's a fine name for the little guy."

Audrey placed the baby back in his dirty crib unable to find anything clean in the tent. "Good night, David." She smiled down at him and waited for him to fall asleep. Then she and Eddie moved two mattresses next to the cradle to settle down for the night.

"I'm going to peek out the tent flap and see if we have a guard." He went over and opened the flap.

"One of those cutthroats is right outside with a rifle. We're not going anywhere tonight."

He moved back to the mattresses and settled down. "It's going to be okay, Audrey. We will figure something out. Just wait till tomorrow morning."

"I know. I sense someone's watching over us, and I'm not feeling as afraid. Poor little David. Could we have been sent to rescue him?"

"From these cutthroats? That's a thought." Eddie turned off his flashlight and lay in the dark thinking. Who was this child, and what did these thieves want with him? Could they have been sent to rescue him?

He looked over at Audrey in the dark. "Good night."

"Good night, Eddie. Glad we're in this together. Maybe we'll do some good while we're here."

As Eddie settled deeper into his mattress, and was falling asleep, he decided the putrid odor filling the tent wasn't that bad after all.

Chapter Four

The Escape

Whem Audrey awoke, she jumped up and made a circle inside the tent. Dust and dirt covered everything like a blanket. *Where am I? And what's that smell? It's awful.* Then she remembered the baby. Walking up to the crib, she saw he was sleeping soundly, and breathed a sigh of relief. *Oh good, you're doing fine.*

Eddie stirred and stood up beside her, looking very sleepy and relaxed.

Feeling irritated, she thought: *How can he be so calm in this situation?*

Hearing a commotion outside, she followed Eddie to the tent door. As the flap opened, she saw the bandits packing up tents, stoves, anything they could carry, and placing the items onto the backs of horses and goats. It looked as if they were pulling up camp and getting ready to move again. No one was watching their tent.

Audrey thought of the harsh, hot sand and wondered how the tiny baby would survive in these severe conditions. Then she remembered: little David had been there longer than she or her brother.

"Well, it's now or never." Audrey looked at Eddie and pointed to the baby. "We've got to get David out of here and fast. He may look healthy, but how long can he stand this heat? I can't stand it, and I've only been here one day."

"Yeah! I was thinking the same thing. But I had a weird experience last night. I woke up in the middle of the night and decided to peak outside the tent flap. The guard was still there." Eddie pointed up. "But looking into the night sky, I noticed the stars were shining unusually bright. This sounds weird, but one of the stars seemed to grow brighter than the others and I thought I heard, *Don't worry. I am with you, and I'll help you.*

"That's so strange. I had the same feeling last night after we were kidnapped, on the ride to this camp-site." Audrey felt chills running down her arms. "Something up there's watching over us."

She walked to the door flap and peeked out cautiously. "Still no one outside our tent. It looks like they are heading in the opposite direction of the old tree, and that's our way back to our world."

"That's bothered me since the door slammed last night." Eddie looked down and sighed. "Someone up in the night sky said they'd help us, so I'm going to believe that and take a chance. We need to leave right now. Are you with me?"

"What are you planning?"

She watched as he went over to the filthy crib. The baby was quiet when he picked him up.

"Wait a minute." Audrey moved over to the crib, grabbed a filthy, threadbare blanket and handed it to Eddie. She rummaged in the ice chest and pulled out several bottles of goat's milk and put them in a dirty sack that she had found lying nearby.

Eddie nodded. "Okay, let's go."

She followed him and the baby out the door flap. There was so much commotion in the encampment that no one saw a boy, a girl, and a baby run behind the tents.

"So far so good." Eddie was breathing hard.

Audrey's stomach felt empty and tight (too bad they didn't have break-fast). She followed Eddie out from behind the tent and noticed he was studying the sand near them. "What are you doing?"

"I'm looking for hoof prints in the sand to show me the direction back to the tree and home."

As they moved away from the noisy camp, Audrey noticed a horse that had become separated from the other horses. It was saddled and ready to ride. Eddie noticed it too.

He nudged Audrey and pointed. "That voice said he'd help us. Now look: a horse right here, saddled and ready." He scrambled up the side of the horse using the stirrup clumsily, and then motioned for Audrey to hand him the baby. When little David was settled in front, Eddie extended a hand and helped pull her into the saddle behind him.

Finally, he handed the baby back to her. "You ready?"

"Wait. Okay, now I have a good hold on David. Go!"

Eddie dug his heels into the side of the horse and held onto the reins. For a moment, the animal took off in a rough trot but then settled down to a walk.

He guided the horse down the trail, and Audrey could make out numerous hoofprints in the sand. She was relieved to know they were going back to the old tree, but they also needed to hurry with the heat raising fast.

"Let's both dig our heels into the side of the horse. Maybe it'll go faster." Eddie dug his heels in and Audrey tried to do the same. This caused the horse to trot for a few minutes, but then it slowed down again, knowing that the rider was inexperienced.

The heat continued to beat down, and Audrey could see sweat trickling off the horse's back. She moved little

David to her side as she wiped her forehead and then his. Looking down into his tiny face, she became alarmed at how flushed his cheeks had become.

"We've got to get out of this heat."

"Keep an eye open for the door," Eddie said, breathing heavily. He looked hot and tired.

Whether it was a trick or someone was helping them, when Audrey looked up, she saw a doorway, in the distance, partially opened, with sand surrounding it.

"I think that's our tree." Her mouth was parched and her lips were chapped. She could barely get the words out. "Don't know how much more heat the baby can take."

"I see the entrance now." Eddie's voiced croaked as he guided the horse in the direction of the door to the old tree, which was a strange sight. There it stood upright, just a door frame with the door open a crack, in the middle of the immense expanse of sand.

When they arrived, Audrey handed Eddie the baby, dismounted first, and then took the baby back, helping her brother get off the horse as best she could.

She guided the horse to the door of the old tree, and they all walked through together. The coolness of the interior surrounded them as sand was exchanged for grass and tiny, delicate flowers on the floor of the tree. Instead of the harsh desert sun, they welcomed the soft light filtering down from above their heads, and Audrey noticed the wonderful scent of flowers, grass, and fresh dirt. The horse bent its head down and began to feed on the lush grass at its feet.

As she collapsed onto the grass floor, she looked up at Eddie. "Got to rest for a few minutes. This is amazing, the smells, coolness, and beauty here compared to the heat of the desert." She turned and looked into baby David's face. It was bright red and had blotches on it that could have been sunburn.

"Oh, you poor thing." She unwrapped the thin blanket around him and gave him another bottle of goat's milk. He drank it eagerly, and she was relieved when the baby's face slowly returned to normal.

"What now?" She looked up at her brother.

He flopped down on the soft ground next to her. "Let's wait a few minutes and get our bearings." Lying on the cool grass, he spread out on his back and rested. All of a sudden, he sat up abruptly and looked toward the door they had entered.

"Did you see that?"

"What?" Audrey turned her head in the direction of the door.

"We need to go, now. We've got to get out of here."

"What did you see?"

"Get up. Hurry!" he yelled as he stood and extended his hand to his sister. Looking at him, startled, she gathered David in her arms and jumped up. Eddie moved toward the other side of the old tree, looking for the gap they had crawled through at the beginning of their adventure.

He looked back at Audrey and the baby. "Somebody's following us— they stopped at the entrance. We need to go now! I can't find the opening. Where is it?"

Audrey felt panic and fear as she

looked for the hole leading to their world. Where was the gap? With no opening, there was no way back. *Can you help us, please?*

She watched Eddie spin in a circle, searching desperately for the hole in the trunk. Gradually, a slit appeared in the wall, opening as if in slow motion until a hole stood before them big enough to crawl through.

When Audrey looked back, she saw one of the kidnappers heading through the door and gasped. Eddie helped her drop onto her knees with David in her arms, and she struggled to crawl through the gap leading into their world. When she stood up outside the tree, relief flowed through her, and she smiled down at the tiny baby in her arms.

"We're home, David," she said. Without pausing to rest, she took a deep breath, gathering her strength to begin to run.

Chapter Five

Back Home Again

When Eddie looked back at the bandit in the desert doorway, he noticed a puzzled expression on the young man's face. The bandit stood in the entrance to the tree for a moment, and then walked back out into the hot desert. He pinched himself as he moved back into the doorway again and stared at the interior of the tree. Finally, he moved slowly into the cool interior, turning in a circle to take in his surroundings.

Eddie paused to watch the stranger. Then he dropped on his knees and crawled through the gap in the trunk of the old tree.

Crawling through the opening, he stood up outside the tree and was relieved to see the familiar open land of home. After the stark desert landscape, the green trees and colorful flowers were a welcome sight.

"Look, Audrey, we're home. Now run!" He grabbed her hand and partially dragged her through the open country.

"Hurry!" He turned, just in time, to see the bandit crawling out of the opening in the tree.

At first, the young man looked stunned by the amount of trees, bushes, and grass surrounding him. But after getting his bearings, he ran toward Eddie with speed that ate up the space between them.

Audrey was having difficulty running with the baby in her arms, so Eddie took him and urged her to hurry. Still, the desert man gained on them.

"Got to hide. Follow me." Breathlessly, Eddie ran to a large tree with bushes surrounding it. Pulling Audrey down, he put his finger over his lips. Silence filled the air, which made it difficult to muffle their heavy breathing after the strenuous run. He strained to listen for the stranger's footsteps but heard nothing. Audrey gave the baby a bottle from the sack, and little David drank from it quietly.

Huddling in the bushes for what seemed like hours, Eddie finally heard footsteps. A man's voice broke the silence. It sounded familiar and reminded him of the voice he'd heard before, saying, *Don't worry. I am with you, and I'll help you.*

"Hello there. Are you looking for something?"

Eddie peeked through the branches and saw a stranger talking to the desert man, who grunted a reply, turned, and ran back toward the tree. Eddie looked at Audrey, put his finger to his lips in the universal sign of silence, and sat very still as he listened to the footsteps fade away.

"It's all right, Eddie and Audrey. You can bring David out. You're safe."

Eddie looked at his sister and shook his head, putting his finger over his lips again. Suddenly, a man's face peeked over the bushes. He had the kindest eyes Eddie had ever seen.

The man smiled. "You can come out now. The bandit's gone."

"But...who are you? And how do you know our names?"

"Don't worry. I am here to help you."

Eddie looked into the face of the man standing in front of him. "Are you the voice I heard in the desert?"

"Yes, and I'm the one who said, *'I'll help you.'*" The man turned to Audrey. "And I'm the one who filled you with peace, Audrey, when you looked up into the desert sky the night you were kidnapped. I have been watching over the two of you this entire time."

"Thank you for helping us." The strain and anxiety began to fade from Audrey's face.

"Yeah, thanks." Eddie felt relief wash over him. "But how do you know our names? And who are you?"

"My name is Joshua. But I'm also called by many other names." He looked down at the tiny baby in Audrey's arms and placed a finger into little David's hand. "We need to get this little one back to his parents. He has an important future and is destined to rule one day."

"Hear that, Eddie?" Audrey turned and smiled at her brother. "I knew there was something special about this baby."

The man looked down at the child and smiled. "Every person is special, but some are created to govern nations."

"What do you mean?" Eddie asked.

Joshua didn't answer but turned quickly and headed toward the tree. "We must hurry and get back to the desert."

Eddie and Audrey looked at each other.

"Well, Audrey. Again, it's your choice. I think we should go home because we've already had quite an adventure. Don't want our parents to worry." Eddie looked at the sky confused, "Doesn't look like any time has passed here since we went into the old tree."

"We need to help this tiny, deserted baby." Audrey had a determined look on her face. "I can't give up on him when he has gone through so much already."

Eddie sat in silence, then turned

to Joshua. "We want to help, but we've been gone a long time already."

Joshua explained, "When you move into or through this old tree, time stands still here. You return home at the same time you left."

"Did you hear that, Eddie?"

Eddie laughed. "Okay, let's help this little guy. I can't let you wander back into that desert by yourself."

Chapter Six

Return to the Desert

Now that they were with Joshua, peace settled around Audrey and Eddie. The tiny baby, David, seemed to feel it as well, and he looked up, cooing as Audrey adjusted the dirty towel around his face.

"I'll go with you through the tree. Then go straight ahead as you turn your back on the door. If you continue straight, always straight, you'll eventually reach this child's parents."

"You're not going with us?" Audrey's voice displayed the disappointment she felt.

"Don't worry. Someone from my kingdom will meet you to help."

Audrey frowned. "Is your kingdom in the desert?"

"No, it's in another realm, but my father and I have laws for those living in this desert to obey."

"Well, the bandits sure aren't obeying your laws." Eddie recalled the smelly camp.

"We allow them to choose whether they will live under the laws of our kingdom or rebel. The thieves have made their choice." Joshua looked around him.

"Now it is time to go."

Audrey suddenly realized they were leaving her pleasant safe neighborhood to go into the hot, blistering desert again.

Joshua took Mike's hand, and Mike put his arm around Audrey and the baby cradled in her arms. Together, they walked toward the old tree and then right through the trunk.

"Hey! How'd we do that?" Eddie kept turning around and looking at the interior walls.

Joshua smiled and said, "Are you both ready? Remember to head straight out from the tree, always straight." He took them right through the other wall, and they found themselves standing in the desert heat at dusk. But Joshua had disappeared.

Suddenly, Audrey heard a high-pitched cry and then several answering howls. She clutched little David close to her.

"What was that?" Goose bumps formed on her arms.

"I don't know, but I don't like the sound of it. Joshua told us someone would be here to guide us. I don't see anybody. Okay, we'll head straight just like he said." Eddie's voice sounded uncertain, but he walked straight forward with confidence that made Audrey let out a sigh of relief.

The howling broke out closer to them and was joined by other voices.

Audrey shivered. "Oh, there it goes again. Those howls are giving me goose bumps. And look—the baby's frightened."

Eddie scanned the horizon

ahead. "It's getting dark. We need to move. Hope we can outrun them."

"Oh no, they're getting closer." Audrey cried. "I hope Joshua's help comes soon." Just as she finished speaking, she saw shadowy shapes moving toward them in the darkness.

She counted fifteen to twenty animals forming a circle around them. They looked like light-gray dogs with bushy tails. Alarm filled her as she realized they were trapped.

"Possibly we can get away before the pack gets organized." Just as Eddie said that, the leader stepped forward.

"You have something that's ours," he snarled.

"So, you can speak?" Eddie replied with shock.

"Don't distract me. Give us the baby, and nobody gets hurt."

"Sorry, but we can't do that."

Eddie looked straight into the leader's eyes.

Audrey whispered, "They can talk, Eddie. They're able to talk."

The leader snapped at them, showing his long, sharp teeth, and the pack began to tighten the circle. Audrey heard low growls as the circle got tighter and tighter. David started to cry. She looked up into the night sky and several stars seemed to wink back at her, and then she heard a familiar voice whisper to her, *Don't worry. I am with you, and I'll help you.*"

Suddenly, a shape appeared in the sky above them, and Audrey realized it was an enormous bird. The bird tucked its golden wings and swooped down toward the circle, sounding like a low-flying airplane. It thundered down upon them at a frightening speed.

The coyotes looked up and tightened the circle. The leader made a quick jump toward Audrey, trying to grab the baby in his teeth.

Suddenly, strong talons grabbed her and whisked her up into the night sky. The sound of howling and shrill whining from below faded away as the eagle flew higher. Being afraid of heights, she closed her eyes and held on tightly to baby David. The wind whipped her body, and the cold air bit at her exposed face and hands. *Don't look down*, she repeated to herself.

Within minutes, she was dropped onto something soft and warm. When she opened her eyes and looked around, she was in a nest, high up in the side of a cliff. It was lined with moss, fur, and other soft materials and quite spacious. She lay down and stretched full length.

When she awoke the next morning, standing in front of her was a large bird with golden feathers on the back of his head. He was dark-brown all over with white at the base of his tail, and his feet were yellow. The enormous bird studied Eddie and Audrey, and then its intense, dark-brown eyes fell on the baby.

"Prince Joshua sent me to aid you in returning the child to his parents. I'm a golden eagle, and my name is Golden Eye."

As Audrey studied Golden Eye, she realized he was much larger than any eagle she had seen in pictures. She knew she was in the presence of a very intelligent and wise bird.

"Thanks for saving us. Where are we, by the way?" Eddie looked over the side of the nest to the desert below.

"You're in my nest in a rock cliff, hundreds of feet above the desert floor." Golden Eye looked down. "The coyotes are moving west now. It will be safe to continue in a few minutes."

"Your nest is lovely and quite warm," Audrey said politely.

The eagle looked pleased and began to fix it up with his beak.

"Yes, I'm rather fond of my home here. Our young ones moved out recently to be on their own. My wife's visiting them now. It's nice to have young ones in the nest again. You are all welcome here."

"How many children do you have, and how old are they?" asked Audrey.

The eagle looked out over the desert terrain. "We have two children. They're both over a year old and on their own, but they live nearby."

Unexpectedly, he cocked his head to the side, and his intense eyes searched below. "Time to move. I'll fly you part of the way, but then you must walk the rest. I can't travel freely where humans live, and we'll be going near a settlement of people."

He studied them with his intense brown eyes. "Ready?"

Audrey looked down at the baby. "Ready, Golden Eye."

"Me too." Eddie nodded.

"I'm going to take off and then swoop down and pick up the three of you."

He dove off the cliff ledge and circled around. Coming in close, he gently grasped Audrey and Eddie in his talons and flew off into the morning sun.

Chapter Seven

The Oasis

Audrey could feel the wind whipping around her as she held the baby tightly in her arms. Deciding to open her eyes, she watched a cloud touch her feet as it floated by below. She looked up at Eddie, who was smiling reassuringly at her from the black talon grasping him firmly.

Her arms started to ache from holding the baby for so long, and she was relieved to see Golden Eye descending to the desert below. As she looked around, she noticed more shrubs and plant life than usual in this area, but it was still hot and dry.

He gently lowered them onto the warm sand. "I leave you now. Over the sand dune in front of you, you'll find an oasis. The child's family is there."

"Thank you for rescuing us, Golden Eye. And thanks for sharing your home too. It's lovely." Audrey gave the large bird a hug. Eddie looked for a way to shake its wing and finally gave up.

"Yes, thanks, Golden Eye, we're

indebted to you." Eddie pointed. "So just up that sand dune?"

"Yes, over that hill. Good luck." As the golden eagle flapped his large wings and rose off the ground, a warm breeze blew against Audrey's face. "Goodbye and good luck" floated down to them from above.

Suddenly, she felt alone again. It had been nice spending time with Golden Eye.

Pulling the dirty cloth farther from the baby's face, she smiled down at him. His features lit up when he saw her, but his little forehead was wet with perspiration, and his face was red.

Heat from the sand rose up and almost choked Audrey. *Have to get him back to his family*.

The sun was just beginning to rise, and long shadows created by the sand dunes cast a desolate feeling over the desert. As she looked at the arid wasteland in front of her, she had an urge to sit on the hot sand and rest, but the temperature made her decide to move.

Golden Eye said there'd be an oasis. Sure could use some water right now. Her lips were chapped from the dry air, and her tongue felt like it was glued to the roof of her mouth. She was sticky, hot, and tired, but she received comfort from the thought that an oasis was out there, somewhere, and it spurred her on to keep walking.

"I can see the oasis, Audrey," Eddie yelled from the top of the dune. He walked back to her and took the baby. "Come on." He disappeared down the other side of the mound.

Audrey scrambled up the hill and gasped. Stretched out below her was a paradise filled with springs, plants of every kind, and birds flying from tree to tree.

She looked at the dusty, hot desert all around her and then down at the green oasis. Palm trees covered the valley below, and two majestic water-falls cascaded down from cliffs high above.

She felt a burst of renewed energy and ran down the sand dune. A large pool of clear water spread out below her, flowing down from the rocks above.

On the far side of the pool, she watched a large tan goat with huge horns curled back wading in the pool with a smaller goat by his side.

Audrey plunged into the cool water. Eddie was already sitting in the shallow part with baby David between his legs, looking wet from head to foot.

The pool was refreshing to her

skin, and she drank deep of its coolness. Eddie brought David over to her,
and she gently set the baby down in
the water, holding on tight to his little
round body. He cooed as she softly
scooped water onto him, and he
splashed in the pool with his tiny
hands and feet.

She splashed her brother. "Well,
do you see anyone here? Golden Eye
said the parents would be waiting for
us."

Eddie splashed her back. "Nope,
but there are lots of birds, goats, and
what looks like guinea pigs hanging
from trees. I scanned the rocks above
and noticed caves behind the water-
falls that we can explore. But I don't
see any other humans."

Audrey looked confused. "How
could Golden Eye have been wrong?"

Eddie scanned the waterfall and

caves. "He may not have been wrong. Give them a little time. Anything can happen when you're traveling in the desert. I choose to believe him and wait." He splashed her and baby David again.

She put her hand up to block the water. "Not much else we can do."

"That's right. Remember Joshua also told us we'd find the baby's parents here." He stood up with the child in his arms and began to move toward the waterfall.

Audrey stayed where she was. It felt good after being hot and sticky for so long, and she sat back in the deep blue pool and soaked. Listening to the chirping of the birds, she turned and studied them. *Hmmm, wonder if they can talk. Golden Eye could.* She watched a group of black birds, with orange-spotted wing tips high up in the palm trees.

A slender, bright-green bird flew down next to her and snapped up an insect. When she looked more closely, she could see pretty blue all around its chin and throat and a thin black line in front of and behind each eye. The little bird lay down on the warm rocks next to the pool as if it were sunbathing and then cracked an eye open.

"Hello there," it chirped in a high voice.

"Hello, my name's Audrey. I was hoping you could talk. Golden Eye could, so I thought you might as well."

"Oh, so you know our good friend, Golden Eye?"

"Yeah, and he sent us here to find someone."

"Human, bird, or animal?"

"Uhhh, human. We have a baby with us and were told to come here to find the parents."

"Hey, Audrey," came a shout from the waterfall. When she squinted, she could barely make out her brother's outline behind the water.

"Come over here. You have to see this."

Oh, bother. She slowly exited the fresh cool pool and walked reluctantly toward the waterfall with the bird right behind her.

There was a path made of rough stones leading up to her brother. He was sitting on a chair in a cave, and it opened up to the oasis with the sparkling waterfall as a curtain.

Audrey went into the cave, looking around, and found ice chests, cans of food, and bowls with fruit and vegetables scattered around. She sat down on one of the rough wooden tables and opened an ice chest. Inside, she found milk, water, ice cream, and many more things to drink and eat.

"Someone must stock this cave daily." Eddie waved his hand across the interior of the cave. "That's a good sign, sis. Means somebody will be coming back." He noticed the vibrant green bird. "Well, hello there. See you met a friend, Audrey."

"Yeah, and he can talk too. Isn't he a beautiful color?"

The tiny bird bowed low. "Let me introduce myself. My name is Bee-eater."

"Eddie, do you think this little bird could help us find David's parents?"

He nodded. "That's a great idea. Bee-eater, we're here to meet the parents of this baby." He pointed to little David. "Have you seen people in the oasis in the last few days?"

"No, but I could fly over the desert and search there for you. I will need to tell my wife where I'm going. I'll be right back."

"Okay, do you mind? We could use your help in getting this little one back to his mom and dad."

The small bird twittered, "Of course. I have little ones of my own. Be happy to help. Let me go tell my family, and I'll be right back." Bee-eater flew out of the cave.

"Well, I'm going to settle down in this cave and take a nap." Audrey turned and looked at the baby. "How about you, David? Would you like to join me?"

Before she lay down, Audrey made a wonderful lunch for herself and Eddie. She also gave David a cold bottle of milk and stroked his head while he drank.

At the back of the cave were clothes for all ages, including little David. There were cots with pillows, blankets, and bed sheets wrapped in plastic. They were very clean compared to the bedding in the kidnappers' tent. Audrey set up two beds on the floor of the cave for her and her brother.

Eddie helped her make a crib for David with bumpers made of blankets rolled up on all sides so he wouldn't fall out. When the baby was finally napping, they both lay down on the clean, soft beds. She sighed with relief and rolled over, falling fast asleep.

Chapter Eight

The Reunion

When she woke up, it took a few minutes to remember where she was. Sunlight filtered into the cave as she looked through the opening. Eddie and the baby were still sleeping, so she got up quietly, stretched, and then walked out into the beautiful oasis. The singing and chirping of birds created a lovely symphony, and the scent of flowers floated toward her.

Several little gopher-like animals lay on the ground, and some hung from the trees around her. A small group of bright-green birds that resembled Bee-eater sunned themselves on the rocks around the pool, while wild goats stood at the far side below the waterfall and caves.

Brightly colored flowers and plants she had never seen before peeked out from everywhere she looked. The contrast between this oasis and the barrenness of the hot, dry desert was startling.

"They're coming! They're coming!" chirped Bee-eater as he flew up to her. "I found them. I found David's parents. They'll be here soon."

Audrey knelt down. "Thank you, Bee-eater. I can't tell you what good news that is."

"No problem," he chirped in his high-pitched voice. "I need to go to my family and friends now. Good luck."

She watched him fly to a small group of birds sunbathing on the rocks near the waterfall. He nestled down next to them and closed his eyes. She headed back to the cave to tell Eddie.

"What's going on?" Eddie walked out of the cave and winced in the bright daylight.

"Bee-eater found David's parents," Audrey said excitedly.

The next several hours were spent eating and splashing in the pool with David. The day went by quickly, and the afternoon sun now cast long shadows. Audrey took David into the cave and lay him down for a nap.

"I'll stay in here and watch him. You go rest, Audrey." Eddie waved his sister out of the cave.

"Thanks. The time's going so slow, waiting." She walked out of the opening and sat down with her back against the rock wall, facing the pool of water. Lying back, she watched the small, furry animals climbing among the tree branches, and began to wonder if David's parents were going to make it that day.

All of a sudden, from over the cliff rock came a small group of tired travelers.

They looked dirty and hot as they pulled off their backpacks and linen robes and jumped into the pool of clear, cool water. They drank deeply of the refreshing liquid and then splashed each other and laughed.

Audrey counted eight of them. After everyone had finished drinking from the pool, she stood up from her half-hidden location and approached the group.

She smiled at them. "Hello."

They smiled back at her, and a man stepped forward from the group.

"Are you the ones with our child?" The man looked into Audrey's eyes hopefully.

"Yes, we are. He's taking a nap now, but he's safe."

"Oh, thank you, thank you." A woman standing next to him let out a sigh of relief, and tears appeared in her eyes. "We were so worried and sad when our son was kidnapped." Tears fell down her cheeks. "How does he look? Is he healthy? Did they hurt him?"

"No, he's fine. We traveled through the heat of the desert, but he held up well. Come into the cave. He's in there."

Audrey took the woman by the hand and guided her into the cave with the husband following. Rushing over to the cot, the mother picked up her child gently. David opened his eyes and smiled at her and his father standing behind her. Both parents huddled around their baby, and Audrey could hear soft weeping and laughter.

Then David's father turned to her. "We're in your debt, young lady. What is your name?"

"I'm Audrey, and this is my brother. We're glad you made it here."

Eddie moved to the front of the cave and extended his hand. "Nice to meet you. You have a special kid."

"It's nice to meet you." The husband spoke for his wife as well. "We've been in despair since our son was stolen from us, but now our joy has returned with him. I'm Samuel, and this is Ruth. Our son is the most precious thing in the entire world to us." Samuel looked over at his wife and put his arm around her.

"Prince Joshua appeared to my wife in a dream and told her the child had been rescued and someone was coming to show the way. We chose to believe the dream if there was a chance our son was alive and safe."

"Joshua told us to bring the child here." Eddie pointed at the baby. "We've been calling him David. What's his real name?"

"We named him David. What a strange coincidence."

"Would you like some food and

drink? This place is well stocked." Audrey pointed to the provisions behind her.

Samuel, the father looked relieved. "Yes, please, if you don't mind. It's been a long journey."

Audrey turned and began to gather a variety of provisions together on top of a rough wooden table. The other members of the group moved farther into the large cave, and everyone sat down to a delicious meal. They watched the sunset, and then each looked for a space on the cave floor to camp out for the night.

When everyone was settled with pillows, blankets, and sheets, Audrey lay down on her bed and turned to Eddie. "It all worked out," she whispered.

"See, I told you Golden Eye would come through."

She looked over at her brother with a tired but satisfied smile. "Joshua really is watching over us. Everything's going to be okay."

"Go to sleep, sis. We're going home tomorrow. Good night."

Chapter Nine

Back to the Desert

Audrey stood at the mouth of the cave and watched David and his parents disappear over the rock face leading out of the oasis to journey back home. She turned to Eddie. "Am I glad to see him back safely with his parents. Guess it's time for us to go home too."

"Was just thinking about that. We're going to need to cross that hot desert again. Hope I remember the way back to the tree."

She turned to Eddie reassuringly. "Joshua and Golden Eye both said to go straight. If we continue back the way we came, we'll find it."

He sighed. "Wish it were that easy, Audrey." Then he smiled. "We'll make it back. Joshua's watching over us."

They moved into the cave to collect the food and water they'd need for the trip. When everything was packed, Audrey left the cave to look for Bee-eater. It was early in the morning, and she found him near the pool, sunning himself on the rocks.

Hiking over the rocks to where he was nestled, she sat down near him. "Thanks, Bee-eater, for finding David's parents. Now we have to go home. I wanted to say goodbye."

"I understand." He twittered happily. "No humans remain. They just come through on their way home. Joshua set up a system for the supplies long ago for those coming through on their way home. Someone comes daily to restock the food."

"Wish I could give you a big hug, but I'm afraid I'd crush you."

The little green bird sat up and flew toward Audrey's face, gently touching her nose with his tiny beak.

"There!" He sang with long strings of musical whistles and chirps.

"How beautiful. I didn't know you could make such a lovely melody. You're quite extraordinary, Bee-eater."

The tiny bird flew to her face again and touched her nose gently and then climbed into the air to join his family. "Farewell till we meet again, my friend." He disappeared into a cave high up on the rock cliffs. Audrey watched him vanish near the thundering waterfalls of the oasis.

Right then, Eddie walked up beside her. "Ready?"

"Yes, but I'll miss this peaceful place and my new friend, Bee-eater."

"We need to get home. It's early, and the desert hasn't had time to heat up."

Audrey nodded as she slowly adjusted the heavy pack on her shoulders. She noticed Eddie was carrying twice as much weight. *He's always taking care of me.*

They climbed out of the cool, peaceful oasis into the dry, dusty desert. The sun was not high in the sky yet, so the heat was bearable.

Leading the way, Eddie walked straight ahead, toward what he thought would lead them to the doorway into their world.

After a long time, Audrey noticed the heat rising, and she was thirsty and tired. The waterfall and cool pool had been replaced by hot sun, sweat, and thirst. This went on for what seemed like hours, and when she thought she couldn't bear to go another step, Eddie lifted his hand and stopped.

They threw their packs down and pulled out water skins. Audrey greedily gulped down the sweet liquid.

"Whoa, slow down, sis. We don't know how long it'll take to find the door. Take it easy with the water."

Audrey looked up into her

brother's red face. Sweat dripped down his forehead, and he looked tired, but he managed a smile in her direction as they lifted their heavy packs one more time. She forced herself to lift the pack onto her shoulders once again.

The monotonous journey continued with the sun glaring in her eyes, the sweat dripping down her face, and the thirst, terrible thirst, starting again. The pack cut into her shoulders, and she stopped several times to adjust it.

Eventually, the sun lowered in the sky, but the sand still radiated heat. Finally, the sun disappeared altogether behind a small mound, and things began to cool down considerably.

After several hours, Audrey began to shiver with cold and stopped to pull a jacket out of her backpack.

Because the thirst was driving her crazy, she sat down on the sand, unable to move. "Need water. So thirsty" was all she could get out.

Eddie's red face smiled down at her. "Go ahead. Take a break. Get a little rest while it's cool. We'll start again tomorrow."

She hated hearing those words, *We'll start again tomorrow*. What if they were still unable to find the doorway? How much longer could they go on? Her face was burning, and her lips were cracked and dry. She drank the rest of the water. Discouraged and weary, she lay down next to her brother and placed the pack under her head.

When she woke again, the sun was glaring angrily into her eyes. As far as she could see was nothing but sand and more sand in every direction.

Her mouth was dry, her lips were burned and she wondered how long she and Eddie had been sleeping in the sizzling heat. The day was already well underway, and her water skin was empty.

She remembered the first night they had been kidnapped. *We are here and will watch over you,* the stars had whispered to her, but there were no stars out now, just a cruel burning sun.

Slowly getting up, she saw Eddie was still asleep, and she shook him several times. He sat up painfully, handed her his water skin, and then shielded his eyes from the scorching sun. The water skin was almost empty, but she took enough to wet her mouth and made sure to leave the rest for him, about a mouthful. They both ate what was left in the packs in silence.

Leaving the empty packs behind,

they slowly started the journey again, and everything was exactly the same as yesterday. The blazing sun beat down, the sweat dripped off their faces, and their bodies were weak from fatigue. *Oh*, thought Audrey. *There is no more water, or food, what are we going to do."*

She realized with horror that they had never walked the whole way in the desert. Golden Eye, the eagle, had flown them some of the distance. How much desert had he covered with them in his talons? She began to choke back tears at the thought. *What if we can't make it back after all?*

The blistering sun finally set, and the sand cooled down again. They lay back and put their packs under their heads, falling into a deep sleep.

Audrey dreamed Joshua was standing over her, trying to tell her something but she couldn't understand him. As Joshua spoke to her, it was hard to concentrate on him with the throbbing pain in her throat and the aching sunburn on her face.

She awoke to one more blistering day of the desert sun baking down on her, and it was difficult to get up this time. Her head ached, her eyes were dry as dust, and her tongue was sticking to the roof of her mouth so she could no longer speak. Her lips felt charred and burned along with the skin on her face and it ached.

She stood up too fast and fell back down onto the hot sand again. It burned her, but there were no tears to shed, and she stood up again with Eddie's help this time. He led the way more slowly. Audrey felt slightly better briefly, but then the exhaustion hit her hard again.

Her eyes were so dry now that

she was having difficulty seeing. Eddie was stumbling forward in front of her although sometimes it looked like he might crumble under the searing sun. They continued throughout the day, walking straight toward what they hoped was the doorway.

Finally, the angry sun set, and they both collapsed to the ground. Audrey dreamed again that she saw Joshua standing over her beckoning her to follow him, but she couldn't stand, and her body ached.

The next morning, neither Eddie nor Audrey moved for a long time. Finally, Eddie forced himself to stand up and with the little bit of strength he had left, pulled Audrey to her feet. Her vision was blurry, and everything that took place around her seemed like a dream. Her body ached, her throat burned, her skin throbbed, and she knew she could not go on.

As the sun was setting, she collapsed onto the hot sand, tried to get up but could not. *I guess we're not going to make.* She crumpled onto the soft sand beneath her, and it felt good to rest at last.

Eddie leaned over her, pulling her arm to try and help her up, but she couldn't move. He seemed to be a great distance away, and she heard him calling her name over and over, but she was unable to respond. Then she felt darkness engulfing her, and she passed out.

Chapter Ten

The Rescue

*A*udrey! *Audrey!*

She must be dreaming. There it came again.

Audrey, Audrey wake up.

It was her favorite voice in the entire world calling her, and she felt safe and peaceful. The blazing heat was gone, and coolness surrounded her.

"Welcome back, Audrey."

She opened her eyes, fully expecting to see her mother. But she looked up into the kindest eyes she had ever seen. Joshua was leaning over her and smiling, and she realized they were in the old tree. Eddie must have found the doorway. She tried to sit up but collapsed back onto a soft bed.

"Whoa, sis, be careful. Looks like you're not ready to get up yet." Eddie was smiling down at her as well, his face red with sunburn.

"W-w-what h-h-happened?" Her mouth was still very dry, and it was hard to get those two words out.

"You're safe, Audrey. I found you and Eddie in the desert, collapsed near the entrance to the old tree. I carried you both inside, and you've been resting here for the last three days. Please don't try to get up."

Joshua put a glass of water to Audrey's lips, and she sipped the cool liquid slowly and felt strength returning to her body.

He began to describe the rescue. "You have your little friend, Bee-eater, to thank for finding you. Several days after you left the oasis, I told him to look for you. He spotted both your bodies from the air, lying in the desert sand, and immediately flew to me."

Joshua put his arm under Audrey and lifted her head so she could drink more of the cool water. "Your faces were burned and blistered from the sun, and every part of your

skin that had been exposed was sun-
burned as well. You were severely
dehydrated and in desperate need of
water."

He lowered Audrey back down
onto the soft, comfortable bed. "I
brought you back to the old tree and
have been ministering to you here ever
since."

Audrey looked from Joshua to
her brother and forced a weak smile,
but it hurt her whole face to make that
simple movement. Weariness flooded
over her, and she fell back into a deep
sleep.

When she awoke the second
time, she felt strong enough to sit up.
Beside her small cot was a little table
with water and what looked like soup.
She drank both greedily and slowly
placed her feet on the tree floor. It was
covered in the softest cushion of grass,

and her feet were soothed by this after spending so much time in shoes and socks surrounded by the burning heat of the desert.

She looked around in silence. No one was inside the old tree. *They must have left for a while.* The tiny, delicate flowers that had been planted around the edge of the inside of the tree were comforting to her eyes. She noticed the walls surrounding her were smooth and dry and softly lit by a source that filtered down from above her head.

Now she remembered, of course, the inside of this tree was much larger than the outside. In fact, it was quite roomy, and she drank in the deep peace that permeated the place. Just when she was getting used to the silence, Joshua and Eddie walked through the wall and stood beside her.

"Hope we didn't startle you." Eddie beamed at her.

"No, I was enjoying the peace and beauty of this tree. You're feeling better."

"Yep, feel great, and Joshua's been explaining some things to me as well. Did you know that he and his father created the desert and the oasis? Also, they were the ones who allowed us to discover this tree and stumble into the desert. They chose us, Audrey, to save that little baby." He grinned down at her. "Oh, and he said they knew where we were all the time. He allows many experiences to take place that we think are bad. He sees things differently than we do and said there is always a reason. He said in the end it all works out."

"And David, he's going to be a great king and rule someday." Eddie reached into a hollow in the tree and pulled out what looked like a bright-red apple. He chomped down on it.

"Oh, and Bee-eater was chosen to help us and Golden Eye. Joshua watched over us the whole time and allowed Bee-eater to rescue us in the desert. He's told me a lot more, but you look tired, so I'll stop."

Joshua put his arm around Audrey and help her lie back down in the cot. "Thank you, Audrey, for all you and Eddie did to save little David's life. My father and I choose many people to partner with us. They experience great hardship to help those around them. But we are always watching over them. They do not lose their reward for their help and kindness." He helped her settle comfortably in the bed. "Rest. Tomorrow you go home."

She responded weakly, "it all sounds so exciting. Glad we could help you, Joshua." She yawned and fell asleep again.

He moved the covers up to her chin and sat down in the chair beside her bed to watch over her.

Chapter Eleven

Home Again

Audrey awoke to the smell of eggs and bacon and jumped out of bed. Realizing she wasn't at home but still in the old tree, she shared a wonderful breakfast with Joshua and her brother. Today they were going home. They talked and laughed and talked again about everything under the sun. And then it was time to go.

Joshua led them through the tree trunk and out into the rural area they had played in at the beginning of their adventure.

"I am glad our parents won't be worried, because of the time thing. Can you explain it again, Joshua?" Audrey looked up into Joshua's face.

"This adventure has taken no time at all in your world. When you crawled through the trunk of the old tree, time stood still in your world."

"I think I understand." Audrey looked confused.

Eddie chimed in. "Well, I know I don't understand exactly how it works, but who cares? Wouldn't have missed this for anything. Thanks, Joshua, for showing us your tree and desert. Oh! And that oasis was fantastic. You did a great job inventing that."

"Yeah, thanks, Joshua, for creating such a great place. The pool's beautiful. Can you tell Bee-eater thanks for us? Wish we could see him again."

"You never know. You may have an opportunity to see Bee-eater again sometime. Both of you did a very brave thing. You were stronger and kinder than you ever imagined you could be." Joshua gave both Eddie and Audrey a hug and then reached into his pocket and pulled out two pens.

"These pens will bring this adventure to life. Write down what happened these last few days and guard these pens well. They'll help you remember."

Audrey took the thin, gold pen in

her hand and thanked Joshua. She gave him a big hug. As he leaned against the old tree trunk, it appeared alive with energy. She had forgotten how unusual the old tree was, and she noticed again how the colors stood out against the other trees in the area.

Eddie moved in the direction of their home and Audrey followed him, waving to Joshua. She turned toward her brother, and when she looked back, Joshua had disappeared, and all that was left of their strange adventure was the old tree.

Slipping her hand into her pocket, she pulled out the gold pen and examined it. They headed toward home and walked through the door just in time for lunch.

Look for the other books in this series on
Amazon.com

The Old Tree Series
Tricia Martin

Sheneau Stanley Pastor
livingfreeministries.org

Tricia, uses stories to share valuable life lessons and underlying important values that kids must have to have successful lives today.

Christy Peters Filmmaker

Love this book. The story takes the reader on an incredible adventure. I love how Tricia was able to incorporate things from the extra-terrestrial (spirit realm) and show how they can be just as real and merged into the lives of those of us who live on the terrestrial plain. Well done and an enjoyable read for child or adult!

Desi d'Amani Artist

Enter the world of imagination, intrigue, and adventure! Old Tree is a door into a mystical adventure where life isn't always as it appears to be and lessons are learned through overcoming. This book invites children to explore how decisions affect the world around them and beyond them and it allows the childlike to re-embrace the realities of the once real but forgotten invisible realm. Step through the door into an adventure that will cause you to rethink the world as you once perceived it.

The Old Tree Series may very well be like a Chronicles of Narnia for this generation.

R. Gutierrez

The Old Tree is a portal into a kingdom where courage, hope and the promise of a new day reminds one of love's enduring presence.

Now available in paperback and e-book

The first book in
The Old Tree Series

The Old Tree

Tricia Martin

THE ADVENTURE BEGINS

The Old Tree…a doorway to other lands and extraordinary kingdoms…a new powerful friend…a great battle rages.

Mike is bored with his summer vacation and meets a new neighbor, Mari. Together, with a loving and powerful friend, Joshua, they crawl into an extraordinary tree and are surprised when they find the Old Tree is a doorway into a wonderful kingdom. When Mike and Mari return home, they discover a terrible battle raging. They must join their friend Joshua in saving their world from their enemy, Sitnaw.

Now available in paperback and e-book

The second book in
The Old Tree Series

The Land of Bizia

Tricia Martin

A VERY BUSY LAND

The Old Tree…a doorway to a busy land, an evil lord, beautiful, underground caverns, and a sinister plan waiting to be discovered.

Mike and Mari find themselves in a world that's on the verge of destroying itself through busyness. With the help of their loving and powerful friend, Joshua, can they rescue the people of Bizia and bring them back to the values, peace, and fun they once knew?

Now available in paperback and e-book

The second book in
The Old Tree Series

The Kingdom of Knon

Tricia Martin

AN UNDERWATER KINGDOM IN CHAOS

The Old Tree…a doorway to an underwater kingdom in chaos, a beautiful princess needing to be rescued…a book that holds the key.

The Book has been stolen! That rare gift from the Creator to the people of the Kingdom of Knon when first their kingdom had been made. Now everything has changed in Princess Aria's beautiful kingdom, and confusion, chaos, and fear rule her land.

Joshua brings Mike and Mari to the underwater kingdom to join with Princess Aria. Together, they must travel into space to defeat evil Sitnaw's plan to rule the Kingdom of Knon.

Now available in paperback and e-book

The fourth book in
The Old Tree Series

The Mild, Mild West

Tricia Martin

A GHOST TOWN AWAITS

The Old Tree…a doorway to a ghost town,
talking quail, and evil Sitnaw prowling around
a town of innocent families.

Mike and Mari arrive in the middle of the night in
front of the Old Tree where Joshua is waiting. They
join Mie, a member of a race of warrior beings from
Joshua's realm, and journey into an Old West town
to help in an important rescue. Young people have
been suddenly disappearing from their families. Mike,
Mari, Mie and Joshua join a group of quail who are
eager to defeat the sinister plans of Sitnaw.

Now available in paperback and e-book

The fifth book in
The Old Tree Series

Into the Night Sky

Tricia Martin

A FLIGHT INTO SPACE

The Old Tree…a voyage into space in a
horse-drawn carriage…a search for a special
hat…a temptation.

Mike and Mari befriend a British boy, and all three
find themselves in the middle of the night on
Philip's street. On Philip's front lawn is a carriage
attached to two fiery horses waiting to fly them
into space to search for an extraordinary hat that
has been stolen from the land of Bizia.

Now available in paperback and e-book

The sixth book in
The Old Tree Series

Arabian Lights

Tricia Martin

JOURNEY TO A BARREN DESERT LAND

The Old Tree…a doorway to a
barren desert…a band of
thieves…an oasis…a lost baby.

Mari's father and his sister, as children,
discovered the old tree for the first time. When
they walk through the other side, they find
themselves in a barren desert. An important
child needs their help to restore his purpose.

Now available in paperback and e-book

The seventh book in

The Old Tree Series

One For All and All for One

Tricia Martin

LANDS AND KINGDOMS IN PERIL

The Old Tree…where they travel through
time…Abe Lincoln shows up as a
child…hope is lost, and they must restore it.

All the worlds, lands, and kingdoms are on the verge
of being destroyed by evil Sitnaw. Joshua asks Mike
and Mari to travel back in time to solve this problem.
They must find Abe Lincoln when he was a child and
convince him to join with them to prevent the
destruction of all they value.

Arabian Lights

Educational subjects to study with your child

Study the deserts on our planet, the animal life, vegetation, kind of people that live in deserts and nomadic life. Study eagles and other birds, especially the golden eagle.

For this book I researched nomads living in desert regions and explored what they eat, drink, wear and their temporary campsites. I also investigated the physical effects on a person lost in a desert. How would the heat, sun and lack of water impact them? I studied several desert oases looking at the animals, birds and vegetation that would live in this habitat. Deciding to have a golden eagle in this book, I researched accurate description, habitat, eating habits and their life.

After raising her own child, Tricia Martin now desires to impact the hearts of children with her fantasy adventures involving a loving, kind, and powerful God who transforms the lives of all that come into contact with Him. She has a Master of Arts in Counseling and belongs to the Society of Children's Book Writers and Illustrators, SCBWI.

She has a passion to see children introduced to wholesome reading and believes books feed the mind the way food feeds the body. The reader joins in transforming lands and kingdoms that have been ravaged by the enemy. The reader will fly into space, swim down to an underwater Kingdom, travel to the Wild West, visit a desert and enjoy many other adventures. Each book has educational aspects that the parent or grand-parent can study with their children.

Made in United States
Orlando, FL
20 July 2023

35313553R00086